Bright
≡**Summaries**.com

2084

BY BOUALEM SANSAL

BOOK ANALYSIS

Written by Lucile Lhoste
Translated by Oliver Brown

2084

BY BOUALEM SANSAL

BOUALEM SANSAL

ALGERIAN NOVELIST, SHORT STORY WRITER AND ESSAYIST

- **Born in 1949 in Theniet El Had (Algeria)**

- **Some of his works:**

  - *The Oath of the Barbarians* (1999), novel

  - *Dis-moi le paradis* (2003), novel

  - *Darwin Street* (2011), novel

Boualem Sansal was born in 1949 in an Algerian village. An engineer and economist by training, he worked as a teacher and consultant, ran his own business and worked at the Ministry of Industry in his country, from which he was dismissed in 2003 because of his criticism of the government. An avid reader, it was not until the 1990s that he began to write.

His works are all related to the culture of Islam, as the author questions the use of this religion today. He is censored in his own country because of his political stance, but has gained notoriety in Germany and France, where he has received numerous awards, was awarded the honorary title of Chevalier des Arts et des Lettres in 2012, and was awarded an *honorary* doctorate at the Ecole Normale Supérieure in Lyon in 2013.

2084, THE END OF THE WORLD

A NEW 1984 IN THE ARAB WORLD

- **Genre:** novel

- **Reference edition:** *2084. La fin du monde*, Paris, Gallimard, coll. « Blanche », 2015, 288 p.

- **1st edition:** 2015

- **Themes:** totalitarianism, anticipation, religion, the single deity, revolt, lies, manipulation of history

Sansal's seventh novel, published in 2015, *2084* is a successor to *1984*, the 1949 novel by George Orwell (English writer and journalist, 1903-1950). In *2084*, the world is formed by a single country called Abistan, entirely governed by submission to the god Yölah and to Abi, his delegate. But Ati, the main character, begins to wonder about this perfect universe. Does the Frontier that everyone talks about really exist? Who are the Regs, bandits relegated to ghettos? Why does Nas, an archaeologist, mention a city that would have existed outside the control of the Machine that sees everything?

Winner of the Grand Prix du roman de l'Académie française in 2015, *2084* echoes the surge of religious radicalism taking place in the world.

SUMMARY

ATI'S DOUBTS

Ati, the main protagonist, does not ask himself many questions about the existence of his country, Abistan, about Yölah, his god, or about Abi, his delegate and prophet on earth. But, hospitalised in a sanatorium to treat tuberculosis, he has plenty of time to observe what is happening around him and, above all, to reflect. This is how doubts about everything around him creep in.

Never before has it occurred to him to question what he has learned so far. But he realises that the Holy War, by which the country justifies sending soldiers across the border, has no real purpose, since the citizens of Abistan don't even know what exists beyond those limits. Worse still, he understands that the religion in which he has lived since birth has gone astray: ritualised to the maximum to prevent the population from believing in any other god than Yölah, it forbids thinking for oneself and locks him into a collective, from which he feels he is becoming a miscreant.

His doubts are reinforced when he meets the archaeologist Nas. The latter has just discovered an ancient city that could have existed before Yölah, which, according to the principles of the Abistani religion, is impossible. Long afterwards, Ati decides to go and find Nas at the government where he works to ask him about his discoveries, but he realises too late that he has walked into a trap: Nas has disappeared, and anyone who tries to contact him automatically becomes a suspect. When he realises this, Ati has already left his neighbourhood, which is forbidden, to go to the Abigouv, the seat of government, where he should never have gone.

He then learns, from meeting to meeting, that his suspicions are justified. Both the religion practiced in Abistan and the country itself are an absurdity, a totalitarian regime that has built itself up by crushing all those who stand in its way. Some remnants of earlier civilisations may have been saved, but have been hidden by the government.

Ati, wanted by all the police forces in Abistan because of the many crimes he has committed, decides to go to the end of his convictions, to find the Border and cross it to see what lies behind. No one knows if he has succeeded.

THE DISCOVERY OF ABISTAN

Before his stay in the sanatorium, Ati was like all Abistanis: his city, Qodsabad, was for him only his neighbourhood, the rest belonging to legend. On his return, he was welcomed like a prince: to have recovered from tuberculosis and to have returned from such a long absence could only be due to Abi's favour. However, there is only one thing on his mind: to pretend and hide his status as a miscreant.

As a town hall employee and with the help of his friend Koa, he manages to investigate. Their exploration of the ghetto is brief and only confirms their distrust of the Renegades living there. But their journey within the government will confront them with the brutal reality of their country.

When the newspapers in Abistan mention the village discovered by Nas, Ati and Koa decide to visit him to understand why the official version is so far from what the archaeologist had told Ati in the past. Leaving the boundaries of their neighbourhood, the people they meet on their journey are surprised by their origin, as they too thought that the city of Qodsabad was limited to their neighbourhood. They also discover caravans that they had never noticed before and that criss-cross the country, dragging behind them prisoners whose identity and destination the young man would like to know.

To escape the police, the two friends are hidden by their protector, Toz. Despite his warnings, they continue their journey to Abigouv and discover convoys of prisoners who have disowned the prophet Abi. Denounced by a man from whom they had asked for directions, Ati and Koa are forced to flee, separately. Ati discovers that he is far from being the only one to doubt the benevolence of the authorities of Abistan and the religion practised by its citizens.

AWARENESS OF THE PAST

As soon as he met Nas, Ati had wondered about a detail that quickly became of capital importance: why does the archaeologist think that the city would have existed before Yölah, if there is no past before the god and the country? Since the Abistanis have no real notion of the passage of time (for them it is frozen, there is no real succession of years or eras, so that they do not know in which year they live), Ati is at first doubtful about these remarks. It is Toz who confirms the archaeologist's version, which corresponds to what he himself has understood after many years of study: the whole country lives in absurdity.

Toz tells Ati that the authorities have, for as long as Abistan has existed, used all their energy to manipulate events to serve the cause of Yölah and Abi. His research has also led him to find a past that predates the year 2084, which he can prove through the trinkets kept in what he calls his museum. What's more, he has discovered that the country has annihilated all other existing civilisations, even the Angsoc dominated by Big Brother (a totalitarian society imagined by George Orwell in his novel 1984), which has resisted him the longest. Despite what he knows, Toz argues that there is no turning back and that Abistan is too firmly rooted in its foundations to be destroyed. Ati agrees and decides to make his own discoveries by going in search of the Frontier and what lies beyond.

During his escape, he is protected by one of the Honorable Ones (clan leaders who influence Abistan's politics), Bri, who invites him to hide in a pavilion in his territory. If a witness then spots him on the mountains of Abistan, Ati disappears without knowing if he has found the object of his quest. As for the country, at the end of the novel it begins to suffer what it has caused elsewhere: suicide bombers who claim to spread orthodoxy come to try to convert the Abistanis and blow themselves up when they are about to be captured, so as not to denounce their sponsors.

THE NAS REPORT

When Ati hides out at the Honorable Bri's house, he reveals that the Nas discovery was accompanied by a much more disturbing document: the Nas Report. Rumour has it that this report contains the details of the archaeologist's discovery of the ancient city.

But Ati is actually the first link in the Honourable's plan to use the report to eliminate his political opponents. Manipulating him, Bri asks Ati to give the document to Nas' widow as a testament to her husband. Meanwhile, Bri makes sure that possession of the document incriminates his main opponents: since the report disavows Abi and his religion, it is a crime to simply keep it. Thus the first Honourable concerned is removed from office, while Bri becomes the leader of all believers and all the provinces of Abistan.

As for the report, it turns out, according to Toz, that it is an invention, rumour having taken precedence over reality. The document that circulated was allegedly produced by Bri's clan. It contained disturbing information about the existence of the ancient village, which only Nas saw in the end: as he disappeared in the process, it is impossible to know to what extent his discovery was real or not. But it was impossible to make this report public without fundamentally upsetting the beliefs of Abistan. And so the country survives: by distorting the discoveries to fit the story it has constructed for itself.

CHARACTER STUDY

ATI

Aged 32 or 35 (he himself does not know exactly), Ati used to be a handsome man, but his illness and life in general have taken their toll on his physique. Tall, thin, with green eyes and a fair complexion, he is hairless, nonchalant, shy and has a graceful manner. Despite these qualities, he was ashamed of himself as a child: his soft, somewhat feminine features set him apart from other boys, but also put him at the mercy of men who indulged their baser instincts with young men. While he completely suppresses this aspect of his youth, Ati has retained a certain curiosity and ability to constantly question his surroundings.

Hospitalised in a sanatorium to recover from tuberculosis, he was away from his home town for more than two years. Nevertheless, when he returned, he was extremely well received and was given good housing and a job as an administrative officer at the town hall.

Ati's family is not mentioned, but he does have one major relationship: Koa, one of his colleagues. It is with him that he implements his plans to discover the Renegades first, then the Abigouv. Although he is a bit naive, he is nevertheless perfectly aware of the absurdities of the Abistani system and tries to find out why they exist.

He is of crucial importance to the plot: by breaking the rules to frequent the Renegades and the other quarters, he exposes the extremely coercive nature of the system and the aberrations that flow from it. In Bri's plan, he is never more than a pawn, and his awareness of what is happening in Abistan does not in any way upset the regime's functioning.

KOA

Koa works at the town hall and meets Ati there. The two men share a passion for the richness of their language, Abilang, and get to know each other through discussions on the subject. Koa is highly respected because his grandfather, Koh, was an important religious figure. Unlike those who betray the religion and see their family disgraced with them, he has given his relatives a good position in Abistani society.

This status almost prevents him from going to the Abiguv with Ati. Indeed, although he does not like the idea of punishing unbelievers, he is given the function of judge in a trial for witchcraft (of a woman who had insulted Yölah) because he is the descendant of a good man. Paradoxically, it is also this event that pushes him to leave, in order to avoid the trial and a conviction that disgusts him in advance.

As curious as Ati is to know what exactly Nas has concluded from his discovery of the ancient village, he accompanies him to the main square of Abistan where both are spotted after asking for directions. He flees in the opposite direction to Ati, as each wants to give the other a chance to survive.

According to Toz, Koa died during his escape, skewered on a stake, and his grave is in his clan's domain. Nevertheless, when Ati goes to pay homage to his friend, he is filled with doubts: he cannot rule out that Toz lied to him in some way, and that Koa is still alive, or that he did not die in the way Toz describes. The articles reproduced at the end of the novel imply that Koa was killed by the chaouchs, the Abigouv officials.

TOZ

Toz is a rather old man. He lives in an atypical shop near the wall surrounding the Abigouv. He has a large number of objects from the xx and xxi centuries. His appearance is not very attractive: he is 20 years older than Ati, short, stooped and has a fragile body. On the other hand, his intelligence and charisma impress the two friends when they meet him.

The narrator describes him as a chameleon who has 'the power to assume the face that suits the occasion' (p. 163). He does not look like the other believers and is the first man Ati and Koa do not see wearing the burni, the garment that normally dresses every believer. Toz only wears it when he goes out in the city, while at home he wears clothes that are unknown in Abistan: trousers, a shirt and shoes.

His house, as well as the cache in which he hides Ati and Koa, is furnished as in the old days (this is what Toz explains to them after his research), with chairs, tables, cutlery, etc. He also knows the name of each of his belongings, although there is no equivalent in Abilang.

Later, he reveals that he has a museum that traces the history of humans before Abistan. He is the only local Ati encounters who has evidence that the world has a history before 2084: after studying the period extensively, he has learned how Abistan came into being and why it cannot be easily destroyed.

He is the one who finally gives the hero the light he needs to understand the truth about their country. He is also the bearer of bad news: the foundations of Abistan probably cannot be changed. So he can only keep the memory of those ancient times that the Abistanis will probably never get back.

NAS

Nas is an archaeologist of the same age as Ati, whom the latter meets on his return to Qodsabad. He has just discovered an abandoned village and returns home to report to his ministry, which is in charge of scripting the facts to link them to the general history of the Abigouv, and to find his wife Sri.

Nas does not appear after this interview. According to Bri's clan, he died in misty circumstances: he committed suicide because he preferred to die than to doubt his faith, then he was cremated and his ashes were scattered in the sea. The most likely hypothesis is that he was eliminated by Abistani officials so that there would be no witnesses left to affirm that this village existed before the advent of the regime.

He is one of the few to have understood that the history of Abistan was built on a lie. His discoveries are disturbing: the ancient village escaped the Great Holy War, but also, and above all, the Apparatus, the government's intelligence agency, which normally sees everything. His findings therefore seriously question the foundations of Abistan. Without revealing to Ati exactly what they consist of, he explains that he has discovered things that are in total contradiction with what the Abistanis learn from a very young age. So he realised that the country's religion was fundamentally untrue.

KEYS TO READING

THE RELATIONSHIP WITH 1984

2084. The End of the World is conceived as a successor to George Orwell's *1984*, both from the thematic point of view and in the chronology of the events described in the novel. In this futuristic novel published in 1949, a civil servant named Winston Smith lives in a totalitarian system, a regime called Angsoc, where the entity Big Brother is the dictator and is loved by all. But Winston, like Ati, is guilty of a "thought crime": he rebels against the regime by breaking a whole series of rules (he frequents the proletarian quarter, has an affair, etc.). Once detected, he is tortured in order to be purged of his evil thoughts. He becomes totally apathetic and ends up loving Big Brother after the announcement of an Angsoc victory. He is probably executed.

 ### THE NOVEL OF ANTICIPATION

The main characteristic of the novel of anticipation is that it takes place in a future and more or less distant time. The worlds presented are derived from our own, and present-day elements are used to anticipate the future: a country has appeared or disappeared, a war has taken place, a power has changed...

In addition to the critique it offers of society, such a genre allows us to project our expectations or hypotheses on the future: George Orwell imagines the Telefon (a device combining television and a surveillance system) at a time when television was far from widespread, and in *2084*, Boualem Sansal starts from today's concerns about radical Islam to imagine a world in which this extremism dominates.

At the end of *2084*, the reader learns that there is a connection between the two novels within the story itself: Abistan destroyed other civilisations in order to build itself, and the last regime to resist it was Angsoc, led by Big Brother. Abistan nevertheless drew on Angsoc's resources to establish its bases, which sheds light on the similarities between the two systems.

- **Abilang is very clearly derived from Novlanguage**, the language of Angsoc in *1984*. It is reduced to the simplest possible expression (most of the time, words have a maximum of two syllables) and is designed to remove any possibility for the individual to question what surrounds him. Novlanguage pursued the same goal through simplified grammar and vocabulary that prevented any possibility of dialogue and reflection.

- **The Angsoc Thought Police are to be compared to the Righteous Brotherhood and the Apparatus**, the former being a group of the most fervent believers, called the Honourable, who have some political power, while the latter is supposed to know everything about the actions, thoughts and behaviour of any Abistani. Nevertheless, the Apparatus seems less effective than its predecessor: while Ati is wanted for his incursion into Abigouv Square, he will never be identified or hunted down for his rebellion.

- **Both systems rely heavily on the effectiveness of the ministries in manipulating the past to fit the current belief.** In 1984, Winston himself works in the Ministry of Truth; in 2084, it is Nas who exercises his skills in the Ministry of Archives, Sacred Books and Holy Memories. The ministries are located in very closed places, in London for the first, in the Abigouv for the second.

- **There is no real awareness of the past.** In 1984, the past can be deleted or reshaped at any time; in 2084, the Abistanis live in the belief that there was nothing before that date, corresponding to the supposed birth of Abistan.

- **One supreme enemy is hated and constantly reviled by all citizens:** Emmanuel Goldstein on the one hand, and Balis on the other. The latter is an entity that never intervenes as such, but serves to demonise its so-called followers by making them outcasts and criminals.

- **A more or less fictitious document circulates in both books.** The *Book* (written by Goldstein) is supposed to be a subversive work circulating among Big Brother's opponents, but turns out to be a Party creation. In 2084, there is a document, the Nas Report, also invented to enable Bri to gain power.

- **Portraits of the leader are displayed everywhere and are intended for prayer.**

These are only the main points of similarity. As Abistan is built on the same foundations as Angsoc, there is no shortage of analogies between the two works and these are apparent from the title of Sansal's work and the author's warning. In 2084 there are also real nods to Orwell's work, as can be seen in the warning "Bigaye is watching you" (p. 32), which is a derivation of the slogan "Big Brother is watching you. (ORWELL G., 1984, trans. by Amélie Audiberti, Paris, Gallimard, coll. "Folio", 2014, p. 12)

THE POLITICAL SYSTEM OF ABISTAN

Abistan's policy is based on several important points:

- an extremely precise geographical distribution. Abistan has 60 provinces, divided into cities and districts, themselves designated by numbers and letters (for example, S21 is the name of the district where Ati comes from). The city where the Abiguv is located is built around the central government, surrounded by a wall and comprising the square where all the negotiations take place, including pilgrimage departures;

- a strong religious background;

- clear divisions between the different social classes;

- regular monitoring of Abistan's citizens by the Core, the watchdog, which rewards good believers and takes legal action against disbelievers;

- bodies respected by all, even if their role is not always clear: the Great Mockba, the Abigouv and its ministries, obviously, but also the Just Brotherhood, the various political clans and the mockbas (the equivalent of mosques) for the religious dimension;

- a suppression of individual freedoms, but also of the notion of time, since the Abistanis have no real idea of the month or year in which they live.

All kinds of manipulations are required for the leaders to consolidate their political power: to pass as the most fervent supporter of Abi in order to mobilise support, to neutralise his opponents, to control the press... In order to conquer the highest spheres, Bri's clan develops a particularly complex plan: To set up a Nas report, which would pass into the hands of another clan, in order to disgrace its leaders and ensure that no opponent would stand in the way of obtaining the highest positions.

The ordinary citizen is hardly ever involved in the affairs of the Abigouv. There can only be four reasons why he has to go there: to pray before going on a pilgrimage, to join an Abigouv administration, to register for war, or to go to the front as a prisoner after converting to the Gkabul (the name given to both the religion and the book that is its symbol).

The people can lodge small complaints, but any challenge to the regime or deviation from the law is heavily punished. Either the offender is condemned in a trial to be publicly punished in a stadium, or he is sent on a convoy to the front.

RELIGION-BASED TOTALITARIANISM

The basis of the Abistani religion is simple: Yölah is the god and Abi his delegate. These are abstract, symbolic entities, but every Abistani learns to admire them from an early age. From there, a series of maxims and traditions were developed to increase the mass of followers and ensure their devotion.

Many people go on pilgrimage on extremely well-marked routes so that they only pass through places recognised by the Apparatus. What counts in this process is not so much the goal reached as the journey made; it is the effort made by the pilgrim that proves the strength of his faith. Some of them die during the crossing, which makes this celebration the fulfilment of their existence.

Another tradition, the Jore, is based on denunciation: anyone who performs his or her Jore, i.e. who reports suspicions of disbelief to the authorities, is rewarded for his or her act. To give an example, a witness who sees Ati giving the Nas report to Sri believes that he can perform a double Jore: one for the crime of adultery (the mere fact of having a private conversation with a married woman is akin to this) and a second to denounce the defector.

Abilang, the country's unique language, is a privileged means of conveying the messages of religion. The law imposes its exclusive use and no word has a large number of syllables (hence the very short names of the characters in the novel, for example) in order to avoid nurturing the slightest capacity for reasoning in believers. The schools, which obviously teach in Abilang, use it to convert children into perfect disciples of Yölah.

The *Book of Abi* records all the words of the god and his delegate, which must be known by heart by believers. Some of them directly govern their lives, as shown by this excerpt, which is put before the eyes of those who are examined by the Core, the supervisory body that questions the personnel of the administrations to judge their faith:

> "I have established committees of the wisest among you to judge your deeds and search your hearts in order to keep you on the path of Gkabul. Be truthful and sincere with them, they are my envoys. It will befall the one who cunningly evades, I am Yahweh, I know all and can do all." (p. 87)

Any occasion is good for praying: several times a day in the mockbas, in front of any image of Abi, or when greeting a prominent member of the religious administration. The purpose of this manoeuvre is to achieve total submission to Gkabul (which means 'acceptance' in Abilang). It is really acceptance rather than submission: acceptance of everything related to the beliefs of Abistan and, above all, the fact that there is no other.

Moreover, the system forces the population to live in the contradiction of an inescapable submission and a will to revolt at the same time. "Submission is infinitely more delicious when one recognises the possibility of freeing oneself, but it is also for this reason that mutiny is impossible, there is too much to lose." (p. 51) Despite the system set up to limit any possibility of reflection, it is impossible for an Abistani not to doubt at any given moment, just as it is impossible to doubt for too long: since existence is entirely governed by submission to the Gkabul, any revolt would result in a total and irreversible loss of possessions, friends, family, even life.

A CRITIQUE OF RADICAL ISLAM

Boualem Sansal, in almost all his works, castigates all forms of religion, and in particular Islam. In *2084*, released at a very troubled time due to the news of terrorism and the rise of radicalisation, he targets this religious extremism which is used to manipulate the masses and make them submit to the power in place.

Of course, this is not a criticism of the religion itself, but rather of the use to which it is put. Thus, when Ati visits the Toz museum, he realises that the religion he knows comes from 'the internal derangement of an ancient religion [...] whose springs and pinions had been broken by the violent and discordant use that had been made of it over the centuries' (p. 251).

Radical Islam is never clearly named in the novel, for a simple reason: "In totalitarian systems you don't name things. You have to use very symbolic, incomprehensible things. The enemy is the enemy, that's all. (SENGLER L., « Boualem Sansal: "2084" le règne de l'islam radical », in *Metro*, 12 October 2015)

The religion has a name, Gkabul, a god, Yölah, and a prophet, Abi, but no one knew them or has a written record of what the real Gkabul would be.

The few articles that conclude the novel, however, prove that Abistan's techniques are beginning to backfire. Foreigners are coming to advertise orthodoxy in the mockbas, inciting young people to take up arms against their country and blowing themselves up when they are about to be arrested, in a manner similar to the methods used by radical movements that claim to be linked to Islam. The authorities call for the denunciation of those suspected of being part of this group, as they did for unbelievers.

It is, of course, easy to identify Islam in the ancient religion that served as the basis for building the Gkabul. The Gkabul and its traditions themselves are an obvious implicit reference to the radicalism that is taking place. By denouncing the absurdity of Gkabul, the author wants to highlight the shortcomings of this deviance so that the reader becomes aware of the danger. However, he does so with a glimmer of hope: the world he describes does not yet exist and there is still time to prevent the worst from happening.

AVENUES FOR REFLECTION

SOME QUESTIONS TO HELP YOU THINK MORE DEEPLY...

- What parallels can be drawn between *2084* and George Orwell's *1984*? In your opinion, why did the author choose to include his novel in the latter's family?

- How can the quote below from the novel *1984* also apply to Ati, Koa and Toz?

> "In reality, there was no way to escape. [...] Clinging on day after day, week after week, to prolong a present that had no future, was an instinct that could not be overcome, just as one cannot stop the lungs from sucking in air as long as there is air to breathe." (ORWELL G., *1984*, trans. by Amélie Audiberti, Paris, Gallimard, coll. "Folio", 2014, p. 204)

- In what way could *2084* be qualified as a novel of anticipation?

- Why can it be said that Gkabul is similar to radical Islam? Justify your answer with elements from the novel.

- Is there any truth in Abistan? How does Ati's reasoning shed light on this?

- The narrator says of the poverty of theAbilang:

> "At the end of the ends, silence will reign and it will weigh heavily, it will carry all the weight of the things that have disappeared since the beginning of the world and the even heavier weight of the things that will not have seen the light of day for lack of meaningful words to name them. (p. 103)

- How, in your opinion, can the imposition of this language lead to such a disastrous result?

- The narrator describes the customs and habits of Abistan at length. What elements in these descriptions contribute to the clear cut between the social classes?

- How is Nas' treatment of the discovery of the ancient village an example of the manipulation of the authorities? Answer with evidence from the novel.

- The Abistanis frequently refer to the Frontier beyond which the territories of the Enemy would be found. But if Abistan is supposed to be the only world, how do you explain that a border exists?

- Given the various articles that close the novel, what assumptions can you make about the future of Abistan?

TO GO FURTHER

REFERENCE EDITION

SANSAL B., *2084. La fin du monde*, Paris, Gallimard, coll. « Blanche », 2015.

BENCHMARK STUDIES

ORWELL G., *1984*, trans. by Amélie Audiberti, Paris, Gallimard, coll. « Folio », 2014.

SENGLER L., « Boualem Sansal: "2084" le règne de l'islam radical », in *Metro*, 12 October 2015. http://fr.metrotime. be/2015/10/12/interview/boualem-sansal-2084-le-regne-de-lislam-radical/

Your opinion is important to us!
Leave a comment on the website of your online bookshop
and share your favourites on social networks!

Ebook EAN: 9782808686723
Paperback EAN: 9782808698122
Legal Deposit: D/2023/12603/1092

Cover: © Primento
Digital conception by Primento, the digital partner of publishers.